SATURDAY, SUNDAY, & SALVATION
25 REASONS FOR SUNDAY OBSERVANCE EXAMINED

SATURDAY, SUNDAY, & SALVATION

25 REASONS FOR SUNDAY OBSERVANCE EXAMINED

DWIGHT P. HERBERT

Pacific Press Publishing Association
Mountain View, California
Oshawa, Ontario

All italics appearing in Scripture
quotations are supplied by the author.

Design by Tim Mitoma
Copyright © 1980 by
Pacific Press Publishing Association
Litho in United States of America
All Rights Reserved

Library of Congress Cataloging in Publication Data
Herbert, Dwight P   1908-
  Saturday, Sunday, and Salvation.
  1. Sunday. 2. Seventh-day Adventists
Doctrinal and controversial works. I. Title.
BV111.H46   263   80-10526
ISBN 0-8163-0355-X

Contents

	page
Introduction	7
How to Use This Book	8

1. "Does it matter which day we keep, as long as we keep one in seven?" — 10
2. "Because the calendar has been changed so many times, how can we be certain which is the seventh day?" — 12
3. "Yes, I know that Saturday is the seventh-day Sabbath of Christ's day, but we keep Sunday in honor of His resurrection. After the resurrection the early church began keeping Sunday in honor of Christ's resurrection." — 14
4. "Did not the church have a right to change the day of worship from Saturday to Sunday? My priest showed me these words: 'We observe Sunday instead of Saturday because the Catholic Church transferred the solemnity from Saturday to Sunday.' " — 15
5. "Almost any time Sunday is mentioned in the New Testament, some religious significance is attached to it." — 17
6. "Christ changed the day of worship from Saturday to Sunday: 'He taketh away the first, that he may establish the second.' " — 22
7. "Christians today go by the New Testament because the Old Testament has been abolished." — 23
8. "We are told in Colossians 2:14 and Romans 14:5, 6 that the Sabbath was one of the ceremonial days of worship that were abolished at the cross." — 25
9. "Surely the few who keep Saturday can't be right, when millions of good Christians have kept Sunday. Besides, what about the great preachers and Bible scholars who tell us to keep Sunday?" — 28
10. "Why is it when I look in my Bible concordance or chain-reference Bible for 'Sabbath' that I am referred to the texts that speak of the first day of the week? Also, the marginal reference on Revelation 1:10 in some Bibles refers to the first day of the week as the 'Lord's day.' " — 31
11. "I have to work six days a week to earn a living, and Sunday is my only day off. The Bible says that a man is

    'worse than an infidel' if he does not support his family.''   32
12. "The days of Creation week were long periods of time, not twenty-four-hour days."   36
13. "Christians are not under law but under grace, and I've been saved! How can I be lost if I don't keep the seventh-day Sabbath?"   38
14. "I have the gift of the Holy Spirit, and would He not show me if I am wrong in keeping Sunday?"   43
15. "The Bible teaches that we should not judge one another regarding one's day of worship."   44
16. "Jesus said, 'A new commandment I give unto you—love.' The Jewish Sabbath was no longer His emphasis."   46
17. "Paul said that 'Christ is the end of the law for righteousness to every one that believeth' (Romans 10:4); Jesus said that He came 'to fulfil' the law (Matthew 5:17)."   48
18. "Only legalists, like Jews and Seventh-day Adventists, try to keep the seventh-day Sabbath."   49
19. "Seventh-day Adventists teach that God gave one law and Moses another. Actually, God gave only one law to mankind."   49
20. "The seventh-day Sabbath was given only to the Jews by God on Mount Sinai; Gentiles were never commanded to keep the Sabbath."   50
21. "The New Testament does not give a single command to keep the seventh-day Sabbath. Is there a penalty mentioned for breaking it?"   53
22. "My family and friends would call me a fool for keeping Saturday instead of Sunday."   55
23. "God gave the Mormon Church a direct revelation that Sunday was substituted for the old Jewish Sabbath."   57
24. "There is no commandment in the Ten Commandments which says that we are to keep the seventh day of the week."   59
25. "Although no biblical command requires Christians to keep Sunday, its observance is his liberty to enjoy."   60

Introduction

Millions of Christians love the Lord and are observing Sunday, the first day of the week, as their day of rest. But why do they keep Sunday as if it were the Sabbath, or even as the *Lord's day,* when the Bible tells us in Exodus 20:10 "the *seventh* day is the Sabbath of the *Lord*"?

This book lists the general reasons most often given for Sunday keeping and then answers them from the Holy Scriptures.

The author wrote this book after more than thirty years of dealing with this subject. While serving as the head of the Twentieth Century Bible Correspondence School (Charlotte, North Carolina), he was responsible for answering the Bible questions asked by students. This gave him additional experience in answering questions relative to whether the Sabbath was Saturday or Sunday.

He discovered that many Christians do not know why they keep Sunday; neither do they know the valid biblical reasons for keeping the seventh-day (Saturday) Sabbath. He was reminded constantly that people really wanted to know the truth about this biblical subject and generally appreciated the opportunity to consider both sides of the question.

How to use this book

First, read the book through. Then, when a friend, relative, fellow church member, teacher, or preacher contends that keeping Sunday is correct, compare his reason against the list of questions or reasons given for Sunday keeping in the table of contents. Turn to the page indicated, and you will find the answer with the Bible verses you need.

Become familiar with all the answers, because the Sabbath-Sunday subject will become increasingly more important and public. You will then be "ready always to give an answer to every man that asketh you a reason of the hope that is in you with meekness and fear." 1 Peter 3:15.

Some may think, "What I don't know, I'll not be responsible for." But this is dangerous thinking. The Bible warns, "There is a way which seemeth right unto a man, but the end thereof are the ways of death." Proverbs 14:12.

The Bible also teaches that we are responsible for all the opportunities we have had to know the truth. "My people are destroyed for lack of knowledge: *because thou has rejected knowledge,* I will also reject thee . . . : *seeing thou hast forgotten the law of thy God,* I will also forget thy children." Hosea 4:6. If we have an opportunity to study God's law and yet we turn away from it in procrastination or rejection, what then? "He that turneth away his ear from hearing the law, even his prayer shall be abomination." Proverbs 28:9.

In spite of the reasons given for Sunday keeping, more than three million Seventh-day Adventist Christians believe that the keeping of the seventh-day Sabbath will be the final test of one's loyalty to God, especially in the days just before Jesus returns.

These Sabbath keepers accept the biblical teaching that when Jesus comes again as King of kings and Lord of lords, only those who, by His grace, "keep the commandments of God, and the faith of Jesus" (Revelation 14:12) will be saved. This means that those who are not keeping the seventh-day

Sabbath at that time will be lost; for the Sabbath commandment, which enjoins the keeping of the seventh day, is one of the Ten Commandments. Seventh-day Adventists have accepted Christ as their Saviour from both the penalty and power of sin. They love Him who has flung open the gates of heaven to all who accept His loving plan for their redemption. They believe that keeping the Ten Commandments is an *evidence* of conversion and of a saving relationship with Jesus Christ. See John 14:15; 15:10; 1 John 1:3-6.

God has invited us to reason things through—not to jump to premature conclusions: "Come now, and let us reason together, saith the Lord." Isaiah 1:18.

Christians generally agree that the Bible alone should be the final authority on deciding Christian doctrines. Let us proceed to the twenty-five most-often-given reasons for Sunday keeping, believing that God will illuminate our minds as we seek His truth.

Does It Matter?

1. Does it matter which day we keep, as long as we keep one in seven?"

ANSWER: This reasoning would be more plausible if God had said in the fourth commandment "a seventh day" or even "every seventh day," but God used the definite article *the*: "Remember *the* sabbath day. . . . But *the* seventh day is *the* sabbath of the Lord thy God." Exodus 20:8-10.

The definite article *the* limits the Sabbath to only one day of the week, namely, the seventh. God impressed this truth on the Israelites in a lesson repeated weekly for forty years. Read Exodus 16.

"Then said the Lord unto Moses, Behold, I will rain bread from heaven for you; and the people shall go out and gather a certain rate every day, that I may *prove* them, *whether they will walk in my law, or no*. And it shall come to pass, that on the sixth day they shall prepare that which they bring in; and it shall be twice as much as they gather daily." Exodus 16: 4, 5.

Notice that when God tested the children of Israel "whether they will walk in my law, or no," He tested them with the Sabbath.

Some, not trusting God for their daily bread, tried to store up some bread for the future, only to find it spoiled on the next day.

But God told them to change their procedure every sixth day, *the day before the Sabbath,* and to gather twice as much as on previous days. They were to prepare it for Sabbath eating on the sixth day because no manna would fall on the Sabbath. The food collected on the sixth day for the Sabbath would not spoil. See verses 23-26.

But some then used the same reasoning as many do for Sunday keeping today—"It doesn't make any difference, just so we keep one day in seven." The record states, "And it came to pass, that there went out some of the people on the seventh day for to gather, and they found none. And the Lord said unto Moses, How long refuse ye to keep my commandments and my laws?" Exodus 16:27, 28.

God was particular about which day was His Sabbath, and He expects His people to be likewise. (Notice that this even occurred before God thundered His law from Mount Sinai, indicating that men were acquainted with the law of God, including the Sabbath, before Sinai.)

Let us read the last section of the fourth commandment: "For in six days the Lord made heaven and earth, the sea, and all that in them is, and rested *the* seventh day: wherefore the Lord blessed *the* sabbath day, and hallowed it." Exodus 20:11.

The seventh day of Creation week was the first Sabbath on earth, beginning the seven-day cycle that God referred to in the fourth commandment. The Sabbath day of the Ten Commandments, *the* seventh day of each weekly cycle since Creation, is the only day in the week that is especially "blessed" and "sanctified." Genesis 2:3.

We may search the Bible, but not a single text will be found where God "blessed" Sunday. Sunday is considered by God as one of the ordinary work days. "*Six* days shalt thou labor and do all thy work, but *the* seventh day is *the* Sabbath of the Lord thy God."

If it makes a difference with God, it should make a difference with us.

The Calendar Change

2. "Because the calendar has been changed so many times, how can we be certain which is the seventh day?"

ANSWER: No question about it—the calendar has been changed. But not the weekly cycle! Would God command His people to keep the seventh-day Sabbath without telling them which day was the seventh? No, calendar changes have not altered the weekly cycle; and God is not asking the impossible from His people today.

No one today questions which day of the week was the Sabbath in Christ's time. We still celebrate the day of His crucifixion and call it Good Friday. Luke said, "That day was the preparation, and the sabbath drew on." Luke 23:54. The Sabbath was Saturday. Luke stated that the women who had prepared "spices and ointments" for our Lord's burial "rested the sabbath day according to the commandment." Luke 23:56. From Sinai to Calvary no days had been lost; no confusion had developed as to which day was the Sabbath "according to the commandment."

Further, Luke tells us that Jesus was resurrected "upon the first day of the week." Luke 24:1. Easter Sunday is always on the first day of the week because no one questions the fact that Jesus arose on the day after the seventh day, which is the Sabbath "according to the commandment."

Therefore, in Christ's day, Saturday was the Sabbath of the Ten Commandments, and Sunday was the first day of the week.

The question is: What has happened to the weekly cycle since Christ's day? Did something happen to alter the weekly cycle when the western world changed from the Julian calendar to the Gregorian? The following is a letter from the Royal Greenwich Observatory:

Royal Greenwich Observatory,
Herstmonceux, Sussex,
Hailsham, Sussex,
England.

Ref. 1901   23rd December, 1964

Mr. W. W. Stringfellow,
Pastor, Homestead Seventh-day Adventist Church,
1117 North East First Terrace,
Homestead, Florida, U.S.A.

Dear Sir,

In reply to your letter of 15th October, I have to advise you that there is no reason to doubt the statement regarding the unbroken sequence of the week as far as reliable records go.

Secondly, it is certain that the introduction of the Gregorian Calendar in 1582 and equally its introduction into the British Dominions in 1752, in no way affected the cycle of the week. Certainly specific provision was made in the 1751 Act that although September 2 was immediately followed by September 14, these two dates were successive days of the week, namely, Wednesday and Thursday.

Thirdly, there is no reason to doubt that present day Saturdays are an exact number of weeks after the Saturday between the first Good Friday and Easter Sunday.

Yours faithfully,
Harold W. Richards
for Astronomer Royal

A Memorial to Christ's Resurrection

3. **"Yes, I know that Saturday is the seventh-day Sabbath of Christ's day, but we keep Sunday in honor of His resurrection. After the resurrection the early church began keeping Sunday in honor of Christ's resurrection."**

Certainly Christ was raised from the dead on Sunday, the first day of the week. Mark wrote, "Now when Jesus was risen early the first day of the week." Chapter 16:9. This same verse in the New English Bible reads, "When he had risen from the dead early on Sunday morning."

However, nowhere in all the Bible are we told to keep Sunday in honor of Christ's resurrection.

The idea that we keep Sunday in honor of Christ's resurrection is thus not scriptural; therefore, Sunday keeping must come under the category of the traditions of men. "He [Jesus] answered and said unto them, Why do ye also transgress the commandment of God by your tradition? . . . This people draweth nigh unto me with their mouth, and honoureth me with their lips, but their heart is far from me. But *in vain* they do worship me, *teaching for doctrines the commandments of men.*" Matthew 15:3-9.

Let us ask ourselves a question: When God says, "Keep the seventh-day Sabbath," and a person says, "No, I prefer the first day, Sunday"—is not this preference a human tradition (or a man-made law) and thus in opposition to God?

Although the introduction of Sunday as a day commemorating Christ's resurrection occurred before the end of the second century A.D., Sunday was not, even in centuries to follow, celebrated as the "sabbath."

Other biblical truths besides the seventh-day Sabbath were also distorted in the early church. Some of this change was an effort by the early Christians to separate themselves from Jewish religious practices. Because the Jewish political revolutions infuriated the Romans, the Christians often were punished with the Jews because of many similarities in thought and practice. The Sabbath was probably the most visible sign of similarity with the Jews.

But this shift of attention to Sunday was also part of a general doctrinal deterioration in the early church. The truths of justification by faith, the nature of man, the nature of Christ, and the authority of the Bible were seriously distorted. The Sabbath, given by God to remind men and women of His creative and sanctifying power, suffered as well.

Paul had written, "For I know this, that after my departing shall grievous wolves enter in among you, not sparing the flock. Also of your own selves shall men arise, speaking perverse things, to draw away disciples after them." Acts 20:29, 30.

Paul also noted that "the mystery of iniquity" [or "lawlessness," R.S.V.] doth already work." 2 Thessalonians 2:7. The rapid decline of apostolic purity testifies to the accuracy of Paul's statements.

The records of the early centuries make clear that the transition from Saturday to Sunday was gradual but never total. George Fisher wrote that in the fourth century A.D., "In many of the Oriental [Eastern] churches the Sabbath [Saturday] was still observed like Sunday, while in the West a large number, by way of opposition to Jewish institutions, held a fast on that day."—*History of the Christian Church* (New York: Scribner, 1900), p. 118.

In summary, nowhere in the Bible is there a command to change the Sabbath from Saturday to Sunday in commemoration of Christ's resurrection. Neither do we find this change to be universal in the early Christian church.

Does the Church Have the Authority to Change God's Law?

4. "Did not the church have a right to change the day of worship from Saturday to Sunday? My priest showed me these words: 'We observe Sunday instead of Saturday because the Catholic Church transferred the solemnity from Saturday to

Sunday.' "—Peter Geiermann, *The Convert's Catechism of Catholic Doctrine*, 1957 edition, p. 50.

ANSWER: The Catholic Church has always felt that it had the power to change God's law, even to the changing of the day of worship. What is more interesting is that most of the Protestant churches appear to go along with the Church of Rome:

"Q. How do you prove that the Church has power to command feasts and holy-days?

"A. By this very act of changing the Sabbath into the Sunday, which is admitted by Protestants, and therefore they contradict themselves by keeping Sunday so strictly, and breaking most other Feasts commanded by the same Church."

"Q. How do you prove that?

"A. Because by keeping Sunday they acknowledge the power of the Church to ordain Feasts and to command them under sin, and by not keeping the remainder, equally commanded by her, they deny in fact the same power."—Douay Catechism (1649), quoted in Daniel Ferris, *Manual of Christian Doctrine: or Catholic Belief and Practice* (Dublin: M.H. Gill & Son, Ltd, 1916), pp. 67, 68.

Ample are the accepted sources which reiterate the church's right to change the Sabbath from Saturday to Sunday. Here, for instance, is one more:

"Q. Have you any other way of proving that the Church has power to institute festivals of precept?

"A. Had she not such power, she could not have done that in which all modern religionists agree with her; she could not have substituted the observance of Sunday the first day of the week, for the observance of Saturday the seventh day, a change for which there is no Scriptural authority."—Stephen Keenan, *A Doctrinal Catechism*, 3rd American ed., rev. (New York: T. W. Strong, 1876), p. 174.

The question, of course, is, Could God's law be changed? No more than God's character could be changed. If God's law could have been changed, then Jesus need not have died.

The following biblical verses declare that God Himself would not change His Ten Commandments, nor would He approve any human change:

"My covenant will I not break, nor alter the thing that is gone out of my lips." Psalm 89:34.

"All his commandments are sure. They stand fast for ever and ever, and are done in truth and uprightness." Psalm 111:7, 8.

"Wherefore the law is holy, and the commandment holy, and just, and good." Romans 7:12.

"Howbeit in vain do they worship me, teaching for doctrines the commandments of men. For laying aside the commandment of God, ye hold the tradition of men. . . . And he said unto them, Full well ye reject the commandment of God, that ye may keep your own tradition." Mark 7:7-9.

"For I testify unto every man that heareth the words of the prophecy of this book, If any man shall add unto these things, God shall add unto him the plagues that are written in this book: And if any man shall take away from the words of the book of this prophecy, God shall take away his part out of the book of life, and out of the holy city, and from the things which are written in this book." Revelation 22:18, 19.

No church has divine authority to change God's holy law. However, God did prophesy that an attempted change would be made by the Roman Church: "He shall *think* to change times and the law." Daniel 7:25, R.S.V.

In summary, we note that Sunday has become a day of worship, not because of a change commanded by God or a precept taught by any biblical writer, but because of a self-appointed authority which has dared to speak for God. Sunday observance is a church tradition, not a biblical commandment.

Did the Apostolic Church Keep Sunday?

5. "Almost any time Sunday is mentioned in the New Testament, some religious significance is attached to it."

ANSWER: Let us examine all the scriptures in the New Testament which refer to the first day of the week, or Sunday, and see whether the disciples began keeping Sunday in honor of Christ's resurrection or for any other reason. If a group of Jewish Christians in Jerusalem, or anywhere else, made such a change, there surely should be something in the New Testament about it.

a. "In the end of the sabbath, as it began to dawn toward the first day of the week, came Mary Magdalene and the other Mary to see the sepulchre." Matthew 28:1.

Some have said that "in the end of the sabbath" refers to the termination of the significance heretofore given to the seventh-day Sabbath. This assumption is obviously unwarranted. Let us read the same text in the Revised Standard Version, "Now after the sabbath, toward the dawn of the first day of the week." The New English Bible, reads, "The Sabbath was over, and it was about daybreak on Sunday."

Nothing in Matthew 28:1 remotely suggests that Sunday should be kept in honor of Christ's resurrection.

b. "And when the sabbath was past, Mary Magdalene, and Mary the mother of James, and Salome, had bought sweet spices, that they might come and anoint him. And very clearly in the morning the first day of the week, they came unto the sepulchre at the rising of the sun." Mark 16:1, 2.

This is a parallel text to Matthew 28:1. Again nothing suggests any sanctity transferred from Saturday to Sunday.

c. "Now when Jesus was risen early the first day of the week, he appeared first to Mary Magdalene, out of whom he had cast seven devils." Mark 16:9.

Nothing is said here regarding the keeping of Sunday in honor of Christ's resurrection.

d. "And that day was the preparation, and the sabbath drew on. And the women also, which came with him from Galilee, followed after, and beheld the sepulchre, and how his body was laid. And they returned, and prepared spices and ointments; and rested the sabbath day according to the commandment. Now upon the first day of the week, very early in the morning, they came unto the sepulchre, bringing the spices which they had prepared, and certain others with them." Luke 23:54-56; 24:1.

This text parallels the previous three. The three-day sequence of Friday, Saturday, and Sunday is indisputably clarified. The Sabbath they observed was the seventh-day Sabbath "according to the commandment."

e. "The first day of the week cometh Mary Magdalene early, when it was yet dark, unto the sepulchre, and seeth the stone taken away from the sepulchre." John 20:1.

Another parellel text that repeats the historical fact that Jesus arose on the first day of the week.

f. "Then the same day at evening, being the first day of the week, when the doors were shut where the disciples were assembled for fear of the Jews, came Jesus and stood in the midst, and saith unto them, Peace be unto you." John 20:19.

Again we find nothing to indicate that Jesus wanted His disciples to begin keeping Sunday in honor of His resurrection. In the words "Peace be unto you," Jesus was not giving them a new commandment to begin keeping Sunday holy. He said those words to quiet their fears, for they were afraid. They were not in that upper room celebrating the Lord's resurrection. Hardly! As the text says, they were huddled together "for fear of the Jews," not knowing what to do with the strange reports of an empty tomb. Mark 16:9-13 says that the disciples generally did not believe Mary nor the two disciples to whom Jesus appeared. The evening meeting was not a happy celebration before Jesus came.

g. "And upon the first day of the week, when the disciples came together to break bread, Paul preached unto them, ready to depart on the morrow; and continued his speech until midnight. And there were many lights in the upper chamber, where they were gathered together." Acts 20:7, 8.

If, as some say, the breaking of bread makes this a proof of Sunday sanctity, what about those early Christians who attended church and broke bread *daily*. See Acts 2:46. In fact, "breaking bread" was a Jewish idiom for eating the daily meals. See Luke 24:35. Whether this text refers also to the Lord's Supper or not cannot be determined.

This "first day" text refers to a farewell service by the apostle Paul before he continued his journey. Bible scholars generally agree that this meeting was held on a Saturday night.

In Bible times each new day began at sunset. In Creation week the cycle began, "And the evening and the morning were the first day." Genesis 1:5.

The Bible states that we should keep the Sabbath from sundown to sundown, "From even unto even, shall ye celebrate your sabbath." Leviticus 23:32.

When does "even" (evening) begin? The Bible answers: "At even, at the going down of the sun." Deuteronomy 16:6. Also, "At even, when the sun did set." Mark 1:32.

Thus, when the sun sets on Friday, the Sabbath begins; when it goes down on Saturday, the Sabbath is over.

This point is clarified in The New English Bible, "On the Saturday night, in our assembly for the breaking of bread, Paul, who was to leave next day, addressed them, and went on speaking until midnight." Acts 20:7.

Then, in the daylight hours of Sunday, Paul continued his long journey by foot to Assos. Verses 13, 14.

No particular sacredness is here attached to Sunday merely because a religious service was held. Paul held many meetings with church members during his travels as occasions permitted. His sermon recorded in Acts 20:18-35, one of his most important, was probably preached on the following Wednesday. But Wednesday was not a holy day merely because a sacred meeting was held.

In summary, we have a glimpse in Acts 20 of Paul's busy missionary schedule. He preached often to church groups, whenever possible. The farewell meeting on Saturday night, coupled with a communal meal, was the church's last opportunity to hear Paul before he left on Sunday on his thirty-five mile walk.

h. "Upon the first day of the week let every one of you lay by him in store, as God hath prospered him, that there be no gatherings when I come." 1 Corinthians 16:2.

"By him" literally means "by himself," and it is equivalent in English to our idiom "at home."

Here Paul is telling the Corinthians to figure their accounts on the first day of the week (first chance they have had since the close of the previous week) as to how much they had made the week before. At that time, in the leisure of their home, they should set aside something for the offering that Paul wanted to take to the poor at Jerusalem. He did not want to wait for a money-raising campaign after he reached Corinth. Sunday morning was a time for bookkeeping, not worship.

i. "I was in the Spirit on the Lord's day, and heard behind me a great voice, as of a trumpet." Revelation 1:10.

Although this text does not mention the "first day of the week," Sunday proponents often include it as evidence for Sunday sacredness. Notice, however, that the text does not tell us which day was the Lord's day.

As we learned in Reason/Answer Three, some Christians began to commemorate the resurrection of Jesus on Sunday sometime in the second century A.D. At that time Sunday advocates began calling Sunday the "Lord's day."

However, Sunday, or the first day of the week, is not what the Bible calls the Lord's day. The Lord makes clear which day is His. In Isaiah 58:13 the Lord calls the Sabbath "my holy day." In the Sabbath commandment we read: "The *seventh day* is the sabbath of the *Lord*." Exodus 20:10.

Jesus said, "The Son of man is *Lord* also *of the sabbath*." Mark 2:28.

Since Jesus says that He is Lord of the Sabbath, the Sabbath must be the Lord's day. Christ states that He is the Lord of the Sabbath, for He Himself gave the Sabbath law from

Mount Sinai. See Nehemiah 9:12-13 and 1 Corinthians 10:1-4. Since Jesus gave the law, He had a right to say that He was Lord of the Sabbath.

Jesus calls Himself the "Lord of the Sabbath" because He is Creator and Lawgiver. His seventh-day Sabbath commemorates the Creation of this world in six days—the seventh-day Sabbath completed Creation week. No other day than the seventh-day Sabbath is referred to as "the Lord's day."

Some have pointed to Psalm 118:24 as a Sunday reference: "This is the day that the Lord has made."

But what does this verse say? Psalm 118 is a congregational song of praise. In spiritual ecstasy the worshipers sing their joy, flooded with the awareness of God's presence and guidance. But nowhere is Sunday sacredness hinted.

Along with one Old Testament verse, we have examined nine texts that Sunday advocates set forth as "first-day" texts which allegedly prove biblical support for Sunday sacredness. But we found no references to a command to keep Sunday rather than Saturday, no hint of Sunday worship as a Christian departure from the biblical practice of honoring the holy Sabbath of the Lord.

Did Christ Change the Day?

6. "Christ changed the day of worship from Saturday to Sunday: 'He taketh away the first, that he may establish the second.' "

ANSWER: Hebrews 10:9, as quoted above, does not refer to Christ as changing His holy day from Saturday to Sunday. Paul never dreamed when he wrote this scripture that a person in the twentieth century would misunderstand his point. Here Paul states that Christ supersedes the first, or earthly sanctuary service, by His own death on the cross, thereby making unnecessary the sacrifices of animals which pointed forward to the death of Jesus (the Lamb of God).

The new covenant annulled the old. The old was good—but

that to which it pointed is better, much better. The light of the sun is better than moonlight. Those who could not keep God's perfect law in their own strength nor find adequate compensation in ritual or offerings needed a Saviour who would satisfy justice, pardon their sins, and ratify the new covenant with His own precious blood.

Roy B. Thurman, former Church of Christ minister, presents these thoughts clearly in his book *The Sabbath Today*.

"Sunday-keeping could not have been a part of the new covenant, because when Jesus died, He sealed His will, or testament. Nothing could have been added to it afterward. Before He died, He had given the plan of salvation. He had commanded the ordinance of baptism and had instituted the Lord's Supper. He had kept the Sabbath holy and, by His example and instruction, had showed how to keep it. He had not taught or inferred that another day was to be substituted. The inserting of a clause in a will after the testator has died is a criminal act and is punishable by law. Thus it was not possible for any of the disciples by themselves to add Sunday-keeping to the will of Christ after He had sealed it with His own blood."—Page 69.

Is the Old Testament Abolished?

7. "Christians today go by the New Testament because the Old Testament has been abolished."

ANSWER: The words "abolish" or "abolished" are used only six times in the King James Bible. Not once, however, do these words refer to nullifying the Old Testament.

In 2 Corinthians 3:13 the word "abolished" is used and then in verse 14 Paul states, "But their minds were blinded: for until this day remaineth the same vail untaken away in the reading of the old testament; which vail is done away in Christ."

These two verses together have led some to say that the Old Testament (Genesis to Malachi) has been abolished as an authority over Christians. But they do not follow Paul's argument. "The same vail" refers to the same blindness that the Jews had to the meaning of the scriptures that Moses wrote and to Jesus Christ Himself. Jews in Paul's day could not see any more clearly God's salvation plan than the Jews in Moses' day.

Specifically, Paul compared the veil that Moses placed over his face to hide the brightness of reflected glory (Exodus 34:29-35) to the veil that the Jews generally placed over the meaning of both their sacrificial system and the Decalogue itself. The Jews missed the spiritual intent and meaning of God's instruction through Moses even as they missed the purpose of our Lord's mission. See John 5:46, 47.

This "vail" of misunderstanding is removed when one accepts Jesus as Lord and as the fulfillment of the Jewish sacrificial system. Only when one sees Jesus as the Lord of both the Old and New Testaments will the Bible be read correctly. Therefore when the seeker of truth "shall turn to the Lord, the vail shall be taken away." 2 Corinthians 3:16.

If the Old Testament has been abolished, why did Paul advise Timothy to use the Old Testament as "holy scriptures, which are able to make thee wise unto salvation . . . and [are] profitable for doctrine, for reproof, for correction, for instruction in righteousness"? 2 Timothy 3:15, 16. The Old Testament was the only Bible Christians had when Paul wrote these words.

So much in the Old Testament refers to our blessed Lord. Would we want to do away with that? Jesus used the Old Testament and endorsed it: "And beginning at Moses and all the prophets, he expounded unto them in all the scriptures the things concerning himself." "And he said unto them, These are the words which I spake unto you, while I was yet with you, that all things must be fulfilled, which were written in the law of Moses, and in the prophets, and in the psalms, concerning me. Then opened he their understanding, that they might understand the scriptures." Luke 24:27, 44, 45.

Is The Seventh-Day Sabbath Ceremonial?

8. "We are told in Colossians 2:14-17 and Romans 14:5, 6 that the Sabbath was one of the ceremonial days of worship that were abolished at the cross."

ANSWER: These scriptures do not refer to the seventh-day Sabbath or to Sunday. Paul's argument is that these ceremonial offerings and ceremonial days pointed forward to Jesus' sacrifice on the cross. Our Lord's sacrificial death ended the law of sacrifices. God demonstrated that these sacrifices and ceremonies ceased when Jesus died on the cross: "Jesus, when he had cried again with a loud voice, yielded up the ghost. And, behold, the vail of the temple was rent in twain from the top to the bottom; and the earth did quake, and the rocks rent." Matthew 27:50, 51.

Paul reasoned, in Colossians 2:14-17 and Romans 14:5, 6, that if any Jewish Christian wanted to observe these ceremonial days he might. But he shouldn't try to force such practices on any other Christian—Jew or Gentile. Nor should he any longer observe these cultural and religious practices as a religious obligation. The purpose of the precross obligation had been fulfilled in the death of Jesus.

These ceremonial laws concerning meat offerings, drink offerings, new moons, holy days, and sabbath days were abolished, or nailed to the cross. The seventh-day Sabbath, which is part of the eternal moral law of God, was never included in these ceremonial laws.

God makes a distinction between the ceremonial *yearly* sabbaths and the seventh-day *weekly* sabbaths: "These are the feasts of the Lord, which ye shall proclaim to be holy convocations, to offer an offering made by fire unto the Lord, a burnt offering, and a meat offering, a sacrifice, and drink offerings, every thing upon his day: *beside the sabbaths of the Lord.*" Leviticus 23:37, 38.

Christian Jews may have looked upon such deeply rooted days as Feast of Tabernacles and Feast of Weeks as we do "holidays" today. If I say I like Thanksgiving Day better than I like Independence Day (the Fourth of July) I am esteeming one day above another. This is a personal choice and proper, and that is what Romans 14:5, 6 is referring to. The Christian Jew had the right to observe any feast day he chose—but not out of the sense of religious obligation. However, the Christian Jew or Gentile never had the option not to esteem the weekly Sabbath.

Before the cross, Jewish holy days were to be observed in addition to the weekly Sabbath given at Creation. For example, let us read Leviticus 23:24: "Speak unto the children of Israel, saying, In the seventh month, in the first day of the month, shall ye have a sabbath, a memorial of blowing of trumpets, an holy convocation." Seven of these yearly sabbaths are recorded in Leviticus 23. Each of the sabbaths fell on different days of the week as the years passed, even as our New Year's Day or birthdays do in our calendars.

But these ceremonial sabbath days were abolished at the cross. Not so with the Sabbath of the Lord. The seventh-day Sabbath was not ceremonial in nature but moral and a part of God's moral law.

You say, "What is the difference between moral and ceremonial laws?" Moral laws such as the Ten Commandments have to do with the right conduct of men, women, and children. Ceremonial laws are concerned with symbolic acts of worship.

The seventh-day Sabbath is an example of a moral law for several reasons: First, it is embedded in the heart of the moral law, the Ten Commandments. For interest's sake only we note that, in the King James Version, 297 words are used to set forth the Decalogue (Ten Commandments). The word "is" in the fourth (Sabbath) commandment is in the middle of the moral law of God, 148 words precede "is" and 148 words follow. "The seventh day *is* the sabbath." Not has been, will be, or ought to be, but that little everlasting "is" is still there.

The Sabbath commandment is a moral law; for if we honor

Him as both our Creator and sanctifying Redeemer, we reveal our love for Him. Is it not moral to love God? Is it not moral not to have any gods before Him, not to bow down to images, not to take His name in vain, etc.? If we love God with all our hearts, we will keep the first four laws of the ten commandments; if we love both God and our fellowmen, we will keep the last six of the ten. Is not love to *God* and *man* a moral act?

God gave the weekly Sabbath as a precious gift to man; "The sabbath was made for man." Mark 2:27. God knew that man, for many reasons, needed physical and spiritual rest. One was to curb man's ambition which, if not controlled, would distort his values and shorten his life. Therefore God said, "Six days shalt thou labour, and do all thy work: but the seventh day is the sabbath of the Lord thy God: in it thou shalt not do any work." Exodus 20:9, 10.

Protecting life and health is a moral responsibility. Giving proper consideration and rest periods to our employees and servants as well as to animals, as the Sabbath commandment commands, is a moral obligation, certainly not a ceremonial function.

Seventh-day Adventists are not the only ones who believe with Paul that *all ten* of God's holy commandments are holy, just, and good, making them *all* moral. See Romans 7:12.

Dr. Albert Barnes, noted Presbyterian commentator, said in his comments on Matthew 5:18: "The moral laws are such as grow out of the *nature of things,* which cannot, therefore, be changed, such as the duty of loving God and his creatures. These cannot be abolished, as it can never be made right to *hate* God, or to hate our fellow men. Of this kind are the ten commandments; and these our Saviour has neither abolished nor superseded."

John Wesley said: "The moral law contained in the ten commandments, and enforced by the prophets, he [Christ] did not take away. It was not the design of his coming to revoke any part of this. This is a law which can never be broken.... The moral stands on an entirely different foundation from the ceremonial or ritual law, which was designed for a temporary restraint upon a disobedient and stiff-necked people; whereas this [the moral] was from the beginning of the world."—*Sermons on Several Occasions,* vol. 1, p. 221, 222.

Martin Luther, in his *Shorter Catechism,* said, "The moral law is summarily comprehended in the Ten Commandments."—Page 16, 1834 edition.

In other words, it is just as much a sin to break the Sabbath as to take God's name in vain or to lie or steal. James says: "For whosoever shall keep the whole law, and yet offend in one point, he is guilty of all." Chapter 2:10.

Is Following the Crowd Always Safe?

9. "Surely the few who keep Saturday can't be right, when millions of good Christians have kept Sunday. Besides, what about the great preachers and Bible scholars who tell us to keep Sunday?"

ANSWER: We should seriously ponder a statement made by Jesus: "Enter ye in at the strait gate: for wide is the gate, and broad is the way, that leadeth to destruction, and many there be which go in thereat: because strait is the gate, and *narrow is the way, which leadeth unto life,* and *few* there be that find it." Matthew 7:13, 14.

This text bears repeating from The New English Bible: "Enter by the narrow gate. The gate is wide that leads to perdition, there is plenty of room on the road, and many go that way; but the gate that leads to life is small and the road is narrow, and those who find it are few." Matthew 7:13, 14.

I heard a popular evangelist (who had been hired by most of the Protestant churches in a large city to hold a revival) say that all their churches were like little roads merging into a "broad highway" headed for heaven. He told the crowd who came forward at the altar call that they could join any church they wanted to "except the Seventh-day Adventist church, for we are at *war* with them." That comment reminded me of Revelation 12:17: "And the dragon was wroth with the woman, and went to make war with the remnant of her seed, which keep the commandments of God, and have the testimony of Jesus Christ." The preacher says the "way is broad"—Jesus says, "the way is narrow."

At last count there were 268 Protestant churches, all claiming to make the Bible their only teacher. The Catholic Church must be amused at the Protestant dilemma, on one hand, protesting the authority of the Catholic church while, on the other, observing the day that the Catholic Church set aside for its day of worship.

I am reminded of James Russell Lowell's poem "The Present Crisis":

"Careless seems the great Avenger; history's pages but record
One death-grapple in the darkness 'twixt old systems and the Word.
Truth forever on the scaffold, Wrong forever on the throne,—
Yet that scaffold sways the future, and, behind the dim unknown,
Standeth God, within the shadow, keeping watch above his own."

Nothing is right merely because the majority believes it. We should either believe it because it's Bible truth or reject it without further question.

Someday soon thousands now keeping Sunday for the Sabbath will see the importance of following our Lord's example and will have the fuller joy of keeping the seventh-day Sabbath. In that number there will be many sincere preachers and Bible scholars now worshiping on Sunday.

Probably it will be as it was in Christ's day after He was resurrected and when the apostles preached with power: "And the word of God increased; and the number of the disciples multiplied in Jerusalem greatly; and a great company of the priests were obedient to the faith." Acts 6:7.

Many Sunday-keeping preachers accept the Sabbath truth every year. Without investigating to see how many, I can think of preachers whom I know personally from such churches as Methodist, Baptist, Church of Christ, Advent Christian, and Roman Catholic.

I think of the late John Aul, a graduate of a Baptist seminary. Before he finished training, he asked the seminary teachers to outline the Baptist creed so he could "go out and preach it." They handed him a Bible, saying: "This is the Baptist creed; go out and preach it." In studying the Bible he found the Sabbath truth and began to preach it. His seminary teachers were very disappointed and asked him: "Why did you leave the Baptist Church and join a small denomination like the Seventh-day Adventists?" Pastor Aul reminded them that they had told him the Bible was the Baptist creed. "Now," he said with a smile, "I am a better Baptist than you are, for I preach all the Bible."

Because they have never studied the subject, many Bible students are sincere in their belief that Sunday is the Sabbath of the fourth commandment. But the fact that a person is sincere does not always make him right.

The prophets of Baal in Elijah's day were sincere in their religion. They were so sincere that "they leaped upon the altar which was made. . . . And they cried aloud, and cut themselves after their manner with knives and lancets, till the blood gushed out upon them." 1 Kings 18:26-28. However, their sincerity did not make their religion right.

Unfortunately, some Christian preachers will represent the observations made by Ezekiel:

"Her priests have violated my law, and have profaned mine holy things: they have put no difference between the holy and profane, neither have they shewed difference between the unclean and the clean, and have *hid their eyes from my sabbaths,* and I am profaned among them. Her princes in the midst thereof are like wolves ravening the prey, to shed blood, and to destroy souls, to get dishonest gain. And her prophets have daubed them with untempered morter, seeing vanity, and divining [making up] lies unto them, saying, *Thus saith the Lord God, when the Lord hath not spoken.*" Chapter 22:26-28.

Each person must decide not to be blind nor to follow the blind: "If the blind lead the blind, both shall fall into the ditch." Matthew 15:14.

Are Marginal and Chain References Part of the Bible?

10. "Why is it when I look in my Bible concordance or chain-reference Bible for 'Sabbath' that I am referred to the texts that speak of the first day of the week? Also, the marginal reference on Revelation 1:10 in some Bibles refers to the first day of the week as the 'Lord's day.'"

ANSWER: Bible helps, such as marginal references, chain references, concordances, are important aids in the study of the Bible but are not part of the Bible.

An author of these biblical helps would naturally refer the reader to other texts which *he* thought bore on the subject; consequently the reader must prayerfully and carefully check these helps.

The scholar who prepared your concordance and marginal references was, doubtless, a sincere Sunday keeper, and honestly believed that Sunday is the Lord's day.

We discussed the Lord's day in Reason/Answer Three and Four, and we found that the only day that the Bible recognizes as the Lord's day is the seventh day of the week, which we call Saturday. Your marginal reference for "Lord's day" (Revelation 1:10) *should* have referred you to such texts as Mark 2:27, 28; Exodus 20:10; and Isaiah 58:13.

When a marginal or chain reference suggests interpretations or even when a minister is preaching, we should be like the Bereans: "These were more noble than those in Thessalonica, in that they received the word with all readiness of mind, and searched the scriptures daily, whether those things were so." Acts 17:11.

Another principle by which we can discover the truth about doctrine is found in Isaiah 8:20: "To the law and to the testimony: if they speak not according to this word, it is because there is no light in them."

Is Secular Sabbath Work Necessary in Order to Earn a Living?

11. "I have to work six days a week to earn a living, and Sunday is my only day off. The Bible says that a man is 'worse than an infidel' if he does not support his family."

ANSWER: How often this reason is given for not keeping the seventh-day (Saturday) Sabbath!

But people who work only five days a week and have both Saturday and Sunday off often say that Saturday is the only day they get business affairs and shopping cared for.

Will these excuses hold up in the judgment? Must a person work on the Sabbath in order to make a living? We answer by asking another question: Would God give a law that man could not keep—and then penalize him for breaking it?

Approximately three million Sabbath keepers are in the Seventh-day Adventist Church, and I have never heard of even one starving to death. In some instances it may be difficult temporarily to find employment with Saturday off; on the other hand, many employers are happy to hire Seventh-day Adventists. They know that a man who has the faith to keep the Sabbath can be trusted. They know that Adventists do not come to work drunk or absent themselves because of a weekend hangover. They do not kill a lot of time smoking; nor are they sick as often as other people, according to the statistics.

The keeping of the Sabbath is, in itself, a test of obedience and love to God. Sometimes the Lord may allow a person to be tested severely as part of His plan to develop character. Jobs, at times, are lost. But the overwhelming evidence proves that a conscientious worker will probably get a better position in the end, if he remains faithful to his commitment. In the real long run the faithful commandment keeper will receive the heavenly prize.

I remember a young family in Florence, South Carolina, during the 1930s. Father, mother, and three children had learned about the true Sabbath and determined to keep it. The father went to his boss and asked for the Sabbath off, telling him that he could no longer work on God's holy day. His boss said, "Absolutely not! Either you work on Saturdays, or you lose your job."

The next day he and his family went happily to Sabbath School and church.

Monday morning the boss glowered but said nothing. The father worked harder that week than ever before, showing he really appreciated his job.

Friday, he again told his boss that he could not work the next day because it was the Sabbath.

"Go in and get your pay check; you are through," said the boss. "When you get over this Saturday nonsense, your job will be waiting for you."

Months went by, and the family members were happy in knowing that they were obeying the Lord. The father walked the streets trying to find employment. Jobs were scarce during the depression. The family used up all its bank savings. Other firms wanted the man and his skills, but his Sabbath position tipped the management decision to others.

The little family did not tell the church their predicament or ask for help. Finally, they had to sell their furniture in order to eat and pay rent; all they had left was their bed mattresses. They had faith that God would provide work somehow, in His good time.

Finally, one Friday evening, the father called his wife into the bare living room and said, "Dear, what do you think about our situation? My boss told me if I'd give up this 'Saturday stuff' I could have my job back."

"Honey," the wife said, "we haven't gone hungry yet, but I'd rather starve than see you break God's holy Sabbath. Let's call the children in and ask them." Those children echoed their mother's words.

That Sabbath evening the little family knelt in the usual circle on the bare floor, asking God once more to provide daily bread and a job for Father.

While they were still on their knees, they heard a slight knock. Without waiting for an answer a man walked in—Father's former boss. He had heard his name in the prayers of those dear people, and he was touched.

Looking around at the bare room he said: "John, what does this mean?" gesturing at the empty room.

"I haven't been able to find employment since I left the company."

Tears arose in the man's eyes as he said, "Why, John, if I had only known how much your Sabbath meant to you, this would never have happened. Come back to work Monday, and you can have your old job back and your Sabbaths off too."

When John returned Monday, the boss stopped by, saying, "Come by the office at quitting time." He did and was handed an envelope. At home, surrounded by his wife and children, he opened the envelope. To their joy the check enclosed equaled all the back pay for the months the father had been off work.

But that wasn't the end of the story. John's boss became a Sabbath keeper along with a number of the other men. The plant soon closed down on Saturdays. The psalmist had found modern echoes of his words, "I have been young, and now am old; yet have I not seen the righteous forsaken, nor his seed begging bread." Psalm 37:25.

The verse referring to "worse than an infidel" is 1 Timothy 5:8: "But if any provide not for his own, and specially for those of his own house, he hath denied the faith, and is worse than an infidel."

This verse is concerned with laziness in general and caring for elderly widows in particular. Apparently some church members were ignoring their family responsibilities, hoping that church funds would support their relatives. Paul was urging responsibility to known duty—not the violation of duty.

The Sabbath is part of God's Ten Commandment law; in keeping it, by His grace, we show the world that God comes first and that He is able to provide all of life's necessities to those who trust Him. See Matthew 6:33.

We are told that "sin is the transgression of the law." 1 John 3:4. Further, "Whosoever shall keep the whole law, and yet offend in one point, he is guilty of all. . . . So speak ye, and so do, as they that shall be judged by the law of liberty." James 2:10-12.

To make sure that he was not misunderstood, James went on to write, "Therefore to him that knoweth to do good, and doeth it not, to him it is sin." Chapter 4:17. If we break the Sabbath and do not repent, we are guilty of transgressing the whole law and we will be lost. We are offending in more than one point when we do not keep the Sabbath.

A farmer wrote a letter to the newspaper editor, saying he did not believe God would destroy him for breaking the Sabbath. "Why," he said, "I prepared my soil on the Sabbath, I planted my potatoes on the Sabbath, I cultivated them on the Sabbath, I harvested them on the Sabbath, and I have the biggest crop of potatoes around here."

No one seemed able to answer this Sabbath-breaking farmer until a timid widow wrote in to the newspaper saying, "You tell Mr. Jones that God does not make full settlement in October."

For those who know, secular work on the Sabbath is sin, and unrepentant sinners will not be able to stand in the presence of a holy God. Jesus said, "Except ye repent, ye shall all likewise perish." Luke 13:3.

Some believe that working on the Sabbath to care for one's

family is similar to pulling the ox out of the ditch, an act Jesus commends. See Luke 14:1-5. In this passage Jesus was teaching that it was "lawful to heal" on the Sabbath. See also Matthew 12:12. To heal the sick is an act of mercy even as helping an ox which had fallen into a pit was also an act of mercy. It is necessary, an act of mercy, for a farmer to feed, water, and care for his stock every day, even on Sabbath.

If business is rushing or crops are waiting to be gathered in, people often use these emergencies as an excuse to do "laborious work" (Leviticus 23:7, R.S.V.) on the Sabbath. The Lord taught us that we should reverence the holy Sabbath in the *busiest times* of the *year* as well as when it is convenient: "Six days thou shalt work, but on the seventh *day* thou shalt rest: *in earing time* and *in harvest* thou shalt rest." Exodus 34:21.

The Days of Creation

12. "The days of Creation week were long periods of time, not twenty-four-hour days."

ANSWER: If this were true, it would not be necessary to keep the seventh-day Sabbath as a memorial of the Creation week of literal, twenty-four-hour days.

Those who believe the Bible and yet rely on this reason are playing into the hands of the evolutionists. Many modernist theologians are trying to harmonize the theory of evolution with the Bible. Their basic argument is that Creation week involved millions or perhaps billions of years. Of course this argument rules out any particular significance for the seventh-day Sabbath. However, no one who believes the Bible to be an inerrant statement of truth can also believe in the theory of evolution—that man evolved from the lower order of animal creation. God's Word plainly states, "And God said, Let us make man in our image, after our likeness." Genesis 1:26.

The Genesis story describes the days of Creation week as twenty-four-hour periods. The Hebrew word for day is *yom*, and whenever in the Old Testament *yom* is accompanied by a definite number used as an adjective, a twenty-four-hour day is understood. If we are letting the Bible speak to us, the days of Creation week were twenty-four-hour, solar days, as we know them to be today.

When we turn to Hebrew dictionaries (such as Buhl; Loenig; and Brown, Driver and Briggs), these sources know nothing of the "Christian" evolutionist's argument that each day during Creation week consisted of long periods of time. John Skinner, author of *Genesis* in the *International Critical Commentary*, stated: "The interpretation of *yom* as *aeon*, a favourite resource of harmonists of science and revelation, is opposed to the plain sense of the passage, and has no warrant in Heb. usage."—p. 21.

The commonsense approach to the first chapter of Genesis requires twenty-four-hour literal days as Moses knew them and as the modern reader knows them. Each day, for example, was divided into nearly equal parts—a dark portion and a light portion. If each part was millions of years in length, no sense can be made of the story. How could green plants live through millions of years of darkness? According to the record, each plant reproduced its kind. Without light all plant life would have been dead after several months. Furthermore, much plant life depends upon insects to transfer pollen. If animals, insects, birds, etc., were not created very soon after the plants, but came into existence millions of years later, those plants would have been long dead before their pollinators arrived. Such arguments based on biological facts and common sense can be multiplied.

Perhaps the strongest argument rests in the fourth commandment. Here God is speaking: "The seventh day is the sabbath of the Lord thy God . . . : for in six days the Lord made heaven and earth, the sea, and all that in them is, and rested the seventh day." Exodus 20:10, 11. God is not illogical or unreasonable. He did not ask His people till the end of time to keep a twenty-four-hour Sabbath to commemorate a period that lasted much longer than twenty-four hours. More precisely, He did the opposite as He spelled out the simple, true-to-fact reason for the weekly, seventh-day Sabbath: He created the world in six, twenty-four-hour days and rested on the seventh day of that Creation week, sanctifying it for man's worship. Genesis 2:23.

Once Saved, Always Saved?

13. "Christians are not under law but under grace, and I've been saved! How can I be lost if I don't keep the seventh-day Sabbath?"

ANSWER: One of the great modern delusions is the doctrine that once a person has passed from "condemnation" to "justification" he can never be lost, regardless of how much sin or wickedness he falls into.

This kind of teaching has led preachers to say, in varying degrees of intensity, that regardless of what sin a "saved" person may turn to, whether it is murder, adultery, lying, gambling, cheating, impatient anger, Sabbath breaking, or anything that is considered selfish and mean, such sins do not jeopardize that person's salvation. Some have gone so far as to say that a "saved" person can do these sins without repenting and still be saved. Even if the "saved" person sins while drawing his last breath!

The excuse is that the "flesh is weak," that overcoming sin is not possible in this life and that God looks at a sinner's sins differently if he is "in Christ." This reasoning fails to consider texts such as this: "There is therefore now no condemnation to them which are in Christ Jesus, who walk not after the flesh, but after the Spirit. . . . For to be carnally minded is death; but to be spiritually minded is life and peace." Romans 8:1-6.

What difference is there between Protestants who accept any form of a "once saved—always saved" doctrine and medieval Catholics who bought indulgences while continuing in their sin?

The key purpose of our Lord's incarnation is summed up by the angel: "And she shall bring forth a son, and thou shalt call his name Jesus: for he shall save his people *from* [not in] their sins." Matthew 1:21.

Each text that seems to support this erroneous doctrine can be shown to be contrary to context. But in contrast to these few misused texts is the general witness of Scripture, from Genesis to Revelation, such as: "But when the righteous turneth away from his righteousness, and committeth iniquity, and doeth according to all the abominations that the wicked man doeth, shall he live? All his righteousness that he hath done shall not be mentioned: in his trespass that he hath trespassed, and in his sin that he hath sinned, in them shall he die." Ezekiel 18:24.

"When the wicked man turneth away from his wickedness that he hath committed, and doeth that which is lawful and right, he shall save his soul alive. Because he considereth, and turneth away from all his transgressions that he hath committed, he shall surely live, he shall not die." Ezekiel 18:27, 28.

"But I keep under my body, and bring it into subjection: lest that by any means, when I have preached to others, I myself should be a castaway." 1 Corinthians 9:27.

"And ye shall be hated of all men for my name's sake: but he that endureth to the end shall be saved." Matthew 10:22.

"He that overcometh shall inherit all things; and I will be his God, and he shall be my son. But the fearful, and unbelieving, and the abominable, and murderers, and whoremongers, and sorcerers, and idolaters, and all liars, shall have their part in the lake which burneth with fire and brimstone: which is the second death." Revelation 21:7, 8.

"Now the works of the flesh are manifest, which are these; Adultery, fornication, uncleanness, lasciviousness, idolatry, witchcraft, hatred, variance, emulations, wrath, strife, seditions, heresies, envying, murders, drunkenness, revellings, and such like: of the which I tell you before, as I have also told you in time past, that they which do such things shall not inherit the kingdom of God." Galatians 5:19-21.

"Having damnation, because they have cast off their first faith." 1 Timothy 5:12.

These Bible texts in both the Old and New Testaments show conclusively that a once-pardoned (justified, or saved) individual can backslide and be lost. As long as we live, we possess the power of choice. The new earth will be populated with people who have chosen to be loyal to God's way of life as loving, obedient sons and daughters.

John the revelator made it clear, "Blessed are they that do his commandments, that they may have right to the tree of life, and may enter in through the gates into the city. For without are dogs, and sorcerers, and whoremongers, and murderers, and idolaters, and whosoever loveth and maketh a lie." Revelation 22:14, 15.

Above all else we should listen carefully to Jesus, "Not every one that saith unto me, Lord, Lord, shall enter into the kingdom of heaven; but he that *doeth the will of my Father* which is in heaven." Matthew 7:21.

We pause and ask, What is the will of God? Let God's Word answer with words often prophetically ascribed to Jesus, "I delight to do thy will, O my God: yea, thy law is within my heart." Psalm 40:8.

Jesus continued His description of those who are finally saved, "Many will say to me in that day, Lord, Lord, have we not prophesied in thy name? and in thy name have cast out devils? and in thy name done many wonderful works? And then will I profess unto them, I never knew you: depart from me, ye that work iniquity." Matthew 7:22, 23.

This is a sad picture: People calling themselves Christians will come to the judgment thinking they will be saved, but Christ turns them away. Why? Because they did not do God's will with God's law written on their hearts.

But Jesus does not finish with only a dreary story: "Therefore whosoever heareth these sayings of mine, and doeth them, I will liken him unto a wise man, which built his house upon a rock: and the rain descended, and the floods came, and the winds blew, and beat upon that house; and it fell not: for it was founded upon a rock. And every one that heareth these sayings of mine, and doeth them not, shall be likened unto a foolish man, which built his house upon the sand: and the rain descended, and the floods came, and the winds blew, and beat upon that house; and it fell: and great was the fall of it." Matthew 7:24-27.

Doing God's will involves more than wanting to be saved or to be known as a Christian. The wise Christian does, by the grace of God, what God asks him to do. Keeping God's commandments is the loving response of a grateful Christian.

Believing the truth is not enough—we must act on our beliefs. The "foolish" person probably knew as much as the "wise" person, but their ends were eternally different.

Suppose a person believed in baptism but did not choose to be baptized because he thought it unnecessary. He simply says that he is "not under the law but under grace." Romans 6:14. Would that person be excused from the "work" of baptism because he thought he had been saved by grace and was thus now living "under grace"?

This text is one of the first Bible verses used to explain why many Christians do not keep the seventh-day Sabbath. Those who use it in this way accuse Sabbath keepers of being under the law.

Unfortunately, the next verse is often overlooked: "What then? shall we sin, because we are not under the law, but under grace? God forbid." Romans 6:15.

God's marvelous grace saves us from the condemnation of the law but not from its teaching authority. The law is "holy, and just, and good" (Romans 7:12) and when broken by Christian or pagan still condemns, for "sin is the transgression of the law" (1 John 3:4). God has promised not only pardon from sin but also power over sin. That is Paul's argument in Romans 6 through 8.

Suppose a missionary teaches a primitive heathen that he shouldn't keep the old Jewish Sabbath for those who keep it are under the law, using Romans 6:14 for proof.

Later the missionary calls on this new church member and finds him worshiping his old idols. He tells him, "You must not bow down and worship idols, for that is a sin."

"Really?" says the native, "you told me yesterday that Christians are not under the law but under grace. If I should not keep the fourth commandment, why must I keep the first or second? They are both in the same law."

Suppose while you are speeding through a school zone at 60 miles per hour, an officer stops you and says, "Sir, you are under arrest." Why does he say that? Because you have broken the law, you are under the law. But after paying your fine, you may walk out of court a free man; you are no longer under the law.

However, because you are now free again and no longer under the law, does that give you license to speed through another school zone at 60 miles per hour? Did paying your fine for the last offense give you freedom to break the law in the future? The answers are obvious—as long as you obey the law, you are not under the law. When the penalty is paid, you are also no longer under the law. But there is something wrong with a person's integrity if he thinks that obeying the law is no longer necessary. Such people manifest their insincerity and of course will be treated accordingly by the courts.

So it is with God's law. It was made to be obeyed. He promises sufficient "grace to help in time of need." Hebrews 4:16. But we all know that we have disobeyed that law and are surely "under" that law unless He pardons us or He helps us to stop breaking it. Pardon and power is the grace that we all need. We don't deserve it. It is the gift of God.

James said it well: "So speak ye, and so do, as they that shall be judged by the law of liberty." James 2:12.

Although sincere Christians are not under the condemnation of law, they are still under its jurisdiction. They listen gratefully to John's promise: "Blessed are they that do his commandments, that they may have right to the tree of life, and may enter in through the gates into the city." Revelation 22:14.

Guided by the Spirit

14. "I have the gift of the Holy Spirit, and would He not show me if I am wrong in keeping Sunday."

ANSWER: If a person is sincerely living up to all the light he knows, the Holy Spirit will continue to guide him into more light. That is the Spirit's work: "Howbeit when he, the Spirit of truth is come, he will guide you into all truth." John 16:13.

What is the truth we ought to know? Jesus said, "Sanctify them through thy truth: thy word is truth." John 17:17. The psalmist said, "Thy law is the truth." Psalm 119:142.

In other words, anything written in the Bible, anything Jesus has said, is the truth that pertains to our salvation: "But the Comforter, which is the Holy Ghost [Holy Spirit], whom the Father will send in my name, he shall teach you all things, and bring all things to your remembrance, whatsoever I have said unto you." John 14:26.

The Holy Spirit shows us that God's law is the truth. In the fourth commandment of God's law the Holy Spirit points out that Saturday is the true seventh-day Sabbath. "Remember the sabbath day, to keep it holy. . . . The seventh day is the sabbath of the Lord thy God." Exodus 20:8-10.

As we continue to study the Bible, the Holy Spirit will guide us into "all truth." The Holy Spirit will not contradict the Written Word. The Spirit will not tell one person to keep the seventh-day Sabbath, and another the first day. God says, "I am the Lord, I change not." Malachi 3:6. "My covenant will I not break, nor alter the thing that is gone out of my lips." Psalm 89:34.

However, the Holy Spirit will not guide us into all truth if, when shown the truth, we reject it or *disobey* a plain "Thus saith the Lord." Jesus said, "If any man will do his will, he shall know of the doctrine." John 7:17.

We are also told in the Bible that we should "believe not every spirit, but try the spirits whether they are of God: because many false prophets are gone out into the world." 1 John 4:1.

How do we "try" the various doctrines taught by so many differing voices? Test them with the Bible!

"To the law and to the testimony: if they speak not according to this word, it is because there is no light in them." Isaiah 8:20.

We must remember that evil angels as well as good angels exist, and evil angels may appear as angels of light: "And no marvel; for Satan himself is transformed into an angel of light." 2 Corinthians 11:14.

The Bible is still the clearest test of whether a person, an impression, or even an "angel of light" is speaking the truth. The Holy Spirit does not contradict the Bible but helps us to see it more clearly.

We Should Not Judge One Another

15. "The Bible teaches that we should not judge one another regarding one's day of worship."

ANSWER: This assertion is based on a misunderstanding of two texts:

"One man esteemeth one day above another: another esteemeth every day alike. Let every man be fully persuaded in his own mind. He that regardeth the day, regardeth it unto the Lord; and he that regardeth not the day, to the Lord he doth not regard it. He that eateth, eateth to the Lord, for he giveth God thanks; and he that eateth not, to the Lord he eateth not, and giveth God thanks." Romans 14:5-7.

"Blotting out the handwriting of ordinances that was against us, which was contrary to us, and took it out of the way, nailing it to his cross; and having spoiled principalities and powers, he made a shew of them openly, triumphing over them in it. Let no man therefore judge you in meat, or in drink, or in respect of an holyday, or of the new moon, or of the sabbath days: which are a shadow of things to come; but the body is of Christ." Colossians 2:14-17.

These biblical texts do not refer to whether we should keep Sunday or Saturday as a day of worship, or even whether we should eat clean or unclean meats. They refer primarily to the ceremonial laws that were part of the Jewish sanctuary service. When Jesus died, those laws, "the shadow of things to come," no longer were needed; they had accomplished their purpose. See our discussion under Reason/Answer Eight.

The basic point in Romans 14 is that Paul is urging patience and forbearance among early Christians, especially Jewish members, at a time of transition. The concept that all the Jewish holy days and all the traditional ceremonial rites were no longer binding on faithful worshipers after the cross did not dawn overnight. Some saw it clearly, such as Paul. Others more slowly, such as Peter.

Those who hung on to the Jewish religious customs were considered "weak in the faith." Romans 14:1. Paul wasn't condemning them and wanted no one else to mistreat them. But he did urge that each member should be "fully persuaded," sincerely motivated as "unto the Lord."

In other words, some aspects of Old Testament instruction met their fulfillment at the cross, such as the sacrifices and holy days of the sanctuary service. Other aspects, such as dietary laws and tithing, were as valid after the cross as before. All this the early Christians were sorting out when Paul wrote these words. Love, above all else, was his plea as these issues were discussed and made clearer.

The seventh-day Sabbath was not the issue because it was above discussion. The early Christians never had a problem with the weekly Sabbath for the simple reason that it was not "a shadow of things to come," or a type of Christ's sacrifice for mankind.

Paul is simply telling the young church to be charitable with others who may yet be confused regarding the relative importance of Jewish feast days. If some of the Jews observed any of those traditional holy days, that was up to them. We sometimes say that we like some of our holidays better than others. If I say I like Thanksgiving Day better than Labor Day, I am esteeming one day above another, but such preferences do not make one day better than another. Only God can make a particular day "better" or "holy," which He did only once, in Creation week. Genesis 2:2, 3.

The weekly, seventh-day Sabbaths were not shadows of things to come but memorials which pointed back to Creation week. Each Sabbath is a fresh memorial of the Creation of this world and a recurring reminder of God's love and power available for our sanctification. Ezekiel 20:12.

A New Commandment

16. "Jesus said, 'A new commandment I give unto you—love.' The Jewish Sabbath was no longer His emphasis."

ANSWER: If anything is needed in our world today, it surely is love—love to God and love to man, the kind of love that Jesus had. However, we shall see that love is not in contradiction with commandment keeping.

Our Lord's full statement reads, "A new commandment I give unto you, That ye love one another; as I have loved you, that ye also love one another. By this shall all men know that ye are my disciples, if ye have love one to another." John 13:34, 35.

Jesus, of course, knew that Old Testament instruction also emphasized the priority of love. God told Moses, "Thou shalt love thy neighbour as thyself: I am the Lord." Leviticus 19:18. See also Deuteronomy 10:12; 30:6.

What *was* new was the definition of love that Christ's own life had revealed. Never again could men and women settle for human rationalizations and standards. Jesus was showing them a picture of love that had never been seen on this planet.

Yet, the fullness of love was yet to be seen. Only after

Jesus' death on the cross did believers perceive the meaning of His words, "A new commandment I give unto you." Jesus was asking His followers to love each other, even enemies, as He had loved them.

This understanding led Paul to write, "Love is the fulfilling of the law." Romans 13:10. But he wrote these words after showing that only a loving person can keep the Ten Commandments. See Romans 13:9, 10.

Jesus often faced this issue: "And one of the scribes came, and having heard them reasoning together, and perceiving that he had answered them well, asked him, Which is the first commandment of all? And Jesus answered him, The first of all the commandments is, Hear O Israel; The Lord our God is one Lord: and thou shalt love the Lord thy God with all thy heart, and with all thy soul, and with all thy mind, and with all thy strength: this is the first commandment. And the second is like, namely this, Thou shalt love thy neighbour as thyself. There is none other commandment greater than these. And the scribe said unto him, Well, Master, thou hast said the truth: for there is one God . . . : and to love him with all the heart, and with all the understanding, and with all the soul, and with all the strength, and to love his neighbour as himself, is more than all whole burnt offerings and sacrifices. And when Jesus saw that he answered discreetly, he said unto him, Thou art not far from the kingdom of God." Mark 12:28-34.

Loving God supremely and your neighbor as yourself was not a new commandment in terms of time. The scribe recognized that Jesus was quoting from those Old Testament texts we mentioned earlier.

In other words, if we truly love God, we will want to keep all His commandments. Love doesn't rebel; love seeks ways to please.

John said it clearly: "For this is the love of God, that we keep his commandments: and his commandments are not grievous." 1 John 5:3.

Jesus emphasized it: "If ye love me, keep my commandments." John 14:15. Obeying a loved one is not a grievous matter. Much to the contrary. Love is what the world needs—people who put the will of God and the needs of their fellowmen first.

Did Christ End the Law?

17. "Paul said that 'Christ is the end of the law for righteousness to every one that believeth' (Romans 10:4); Jesus said He came 'to fulfil' the law (Matthew 5:17)."

ANSWER: In Romans 10 Paul is contrasting God's method of righteousness by faith with man's attempts to achieve righteousness by human performance, whether it be ritual religion or externalized law keeping. In verse 4 Paul simply stated that righteousness by faith in Jesus is the only way for man to find pardon and power and thus fulfill the intent, or "end," of God's law. Any other method to find salvation would not reach this end or fulfill its purpose.

From another angle we can say that Jesus as man demonstrated the utter futility of finding righteousness by any other route than by faith. Only by complete dependence on the Father can any man find the grace to overcome evil and self-will. Thus, making Jesus Lord and Saviour marks an end to the abuse of law as a means of salvation.

Jesus summed up the matter well: "Think not that I am come to destroy the law, or the prophets: I am not come to destroy, but to fulfil. For varily I say unto you, Till heaven and earth pass, one jot or one tittle shall in no wise pass from the law, till all be fulfilled." Matthew 5:17, 18.

Jesus did not come to end or destroy the law. On the contrary He fleshed out what obedience ought to be. His life filled full the purpose of the law. His comment speaks for itself: "I have kept my Father's commandments." John 5:10. He fulfilled the pattern of an obedient, righteous person.

Of course, in one sense, as we discussed in Reason/Answer Eight, Jesus did bring an "end" to the ceremonial law, when

He died on the cross. The ceremonial laws expired by limitation when Jesus died because they had accomplished their purpose. The many prophecies which related to Christ in the "law, the prophets, and the psalms" came to pass and were fulfilled exactly as the prophets said they would be. But in all the Bible not a word is written suggesting that since Christ's death, obedience to God's law was either impossible or unnecessary. God's grace makes obedience possible (Romans 6:18; 8:4; Philippians 4:13; Hebrews 4:16), and the moral fabric of the universe makes it necessary (see Revelation 19:8; 22:14).

What Is Legalism?

18. "Only legalists, like Jews and Seventh-day Adventists, try to keep the seventh-day Sabbath."

ANSWER: It seems strange that a person is not considered a legalist if he obeys and honors his parents or considers it necessary to keep nine of the Ten Commandments, but is branded a legalist when he, with a heart of love, decides to obey the Bible Sabbath commandment. Why is this? Is there something about observing the seventh-day Sabbath that gets to the heart of the matter as to whether men and women have any other gods before Jesus?

Seventh-day Adventists do not believe a man is justified by keeping the Sabbath or any other commandment. We believe that we are justified by faith because of the living and dying of Jesus Christ. He alone is the basis for our salvation. But Jesus does expect us to respond in faith, the total response that says Yes to whatever God asks us to do.

Laws of the Bible Given by God

19. "Seventh-day Adventists teach that God gave one law and Moses another. Actually, God gave only one law to mankind."

ANSWER: God is the author of everything written in the Bible. All laws, including the Ten Commandments and ceremonial observances, came from the mind of God and were good for mankind. But there is a definite difference in these laws.

The moral laws, established since Creation, guide a person's conduct, while the ceremonial laws, given because of sin but expiring at the cross, cover religious ritualism and symbolic acts of worship.

Jewish civil laws were in effect as long as the Jewish nation existed. Health and dietary laws were good for all God's creatures, everywhere and in all times.

The issue here, of course, is the contrast between ceremonial sabbaths and the weekly, seventh-day Sabbath.

Briefly, the seventh-day Sabbath was made at Creation (Genesis 2:2, 3); the ceremonial sabbaths were instituted at Sinai, twenty-five hundred years later (Leviticus 23). The weekly Sabbath memorialized God's creative power and the seven-day Creation week (Exodus 20:8-11); the ceremonial Sabbaths memorialized events in Jewish history, such as Passover and the Feast of Tabernacles (Leviticus 23:4-39). The weekly Sabbath turned the mind back to Creation week (Exodus 20:8-11); certain ceremonial sabbaths such as Passover turned the mind forward to the cross, being only "a shadow of things to come" (Colossians 2:17; see 1 Corinthians 5:7). The weekly Sabbath is tied to the weekly cycle; the ceremonial sabbaths were tied to the Jewish calendar and thus were celebrated as one's birthday—a different day of the week each year. The weekly Sabbath will be observed in the earth made new (Isaiah 66:23); the ceremonial sabbaths were abolished at Christ's crucifixion (Colossians 2:14).

Only a Jewish Day?

20. "The seventh-day Sabbath was given only to the Jews by God on Mount Sinai; Gentiles were never commanded to keep the Sabbath."

ANSWER: Deuteronomy 5:1-3, 12, 15 is often used to prove the above assertion: "And Moses called all Israel, and said unto them, Hear, O Israel, the statutes and judgments which I speak in your ears this day, that ye may learn them, and keep, and do them. The Lord our God made a covenant with us in Horeb. The Lord made not this covenant with our fathers, but with us, even us, who are all of us here alive this day."

"Keep the sabbath day to sanctify it, as the Lord thy God hath commanded thee."

"And remember that thou wast a servant in the land of Egypt, and that the Lord thy God brought thee out thence through a mighty hand and by a stretched out arm: therefore the Lord thy God commanded thee to keep the sabbath day."

Moses is here reviewing that marvelous event at Sinai, forty years before. Before Sinai God had made covenants with individuals, such as Noah, Abraham, Isaac, and Jacob. At Sinai, for the first time, God entered into an agreement, a covenant, with a nation. The basis of God's covenants, whether with individuals or an entire nation, was always His law and man's obedience. Genesis 17:1, 2; Exodus 19:5, 6.

Part of the covenant since Creation has been the seventh-day Sabbath. Genesis 2:2, 3; Exodus 16:4-30. The covenant given to the Israelites "in Horeb" included the Sabbath commandment, which connected the weekly Sabbath to their past history and ultimately to Creation week.

Forty years after Horeb, Moses was giving added reasons for observing faithfully the weekly Sabbath. To infer that God gave through Moses a *new* Sabbath law and *new* laws regarding liberality and generosity to servants at Sinai (Deuteronomy 5:14, 15)—that before Sinai God's people were not expected to keep the seventh-day Sabbath or to be kind to servants—is to misread the Bible.

The comparisons seem endless. When God said, "I am the Lord that bringeth you up out of the land of Egypt, to be your God; ye shall therefore be holy, for I am holy" (Leviticus 11:45), should we conclude that only Jews who left Egypt are under this divine command? Hardly. Moses is adding reason to reason as he upholds Sabbath keeping and holy living before the Israelites as their proper response to the Lord's covenant.

Jesus set the matter before us clearly: "The Sabbath was made for man." Mark 2:27. Not for the Jews, not for those who came out of Egyptian slavery only—but for all men, a gift given long before the Jewish race came into existence.

Another text that has been similarly misunderstood as Deuteronomy 5 is found in Exodus 31:13-17: "Verily my sabbaths ye shall keep: for it is a sign between me and you throughout your generations; that ye may know that I am the Lord that doth sanctify you. . . . It is a sign between me and the children of Israel for ever: for in six days the Lord made heaven and earth, and on the seventh day he rested, and was refreshed."

Some observations: The text does not say that the Sabbath was given to the children of Israel *only*. It does say that the Sabbath is a sign that God is willing and able to "sanctify" His people. See also Ezekiel 20:12, 20. Are the Jews the only people to be sanctified? Obviously not.

The Lord had chosen Israel to be His instruments of grace, the people of the covenant. Because they were to be the gathering point for all who would seek the Lord of heaven—Jew or Gentile alike—they were to represent God as One mighty to save. If God couldn't change selfish, greedy, self-indulging Jews into gracious, unselfish people, why should the Gentiles seek Him?

The Sabbath was the outward sign of this inward change. It was the signal to the world that the God of the Sabbath was everything the Jews said He was. When the Jewish nation finally rejected God's covenant, when they rejected Jesus as their Messiah, their commission was given to those who did accept Jesus as Lord, whether they were Jew or Gentile.

Paul wrote, "For ye are all the children of God by faith in Christ Jesus. For as many of you as have been baptized into Christ have put on Christ. There is neither Jew nor Greek, there is neither bond nor free, there is neither male nor female: for ye are all one in Christ Jesus. And if ye be Christ's, then are ye Abraham's seed, and heirs according to the promise." Galatians 3:26-29. See also Romans 2:28, 29.

The Christian today inherits the responsibility once given to the Jewish people. The covenant is renewed to all who make Jesus their Lord. The Sabbath is still the sign of those He sanctifies.

The Sabbath in the New Testament

21. "The New Testament does not give a single command to keep the seventh-day Sabbath. Is there a penalty mentioned for breaking it?"

ANSWER: The seventh-day Sabbath was so obvious in the early Christian church that it was not necessary to emphasize it.

However, Jesus made an observation regarding the Sabbath that became very relevant for Christians who would be living in A.D. 70, forty years after Jesus had returned to heaven: "But pray ye that your flight be not in the winter, neither on the sabbath day." Matthew 24:20.

Jesus told his followers that when they saw Roman armies surround the city of Jerusalem they were to flee for their lives. They were not even to go into the house to get a coat. Jesus knew it would have worked a hardship on His people to flee in the winter or on the Sabbath.

Their prayers were answered, for we do not read of their flight as being on the Sabbath or in the winter. When the Roman legions surrounded the city under Cestius, he suddenly withdrew his troops, giving the Christians an opportunity to escape. They fled to a small town called Pella. Not one Christian lost his life in the terrible siege of Jerusalem. But over a million Jews perished. It does pay to do what Jesus tells us.

Why did Jesus make such a point regarding the seventh-day Sabbath? Because He knew that Christians would still be keeping the Sabbath in A.D. 70.

There is an actual record of 84 Sabbaths kept by the early New Testament Church. Count them for yourselves:

Acts 13:14	1
Acts 13:44	1
Acts 16:13	1
Acts 17:2	3
Acts 18:4, 11	78
Total	84

Some may say, "Of course Paul went to the synagogue on the Sabbath. That was when the Jews met for worship, and only then would he have someone to talk to."

Those who say that are apparently unaware of Acts 13:42, 44: "When the Jews were gone out of the synagogue, the Gentiles besought that these words might be preached to them the next sabbath."

Why didn't Paul say, "No, Christians should meet me tomorrow, the first day of the week, for Christ arose on Sunday and we Christians should meet and honor Him by worshiping on that day"?

What did Paul do on the "next sabbath"? "And the next sabbath day came almost the whole city together to hear the word of God." Verse 44.

Luke, the author of the book of Acts, was still calling the seventh-day of the week Sabbath, in approximately A.D. 63.

In Revelation 1:10 John referred to the Sabbath as the "Lord's day." This was written approximately A.D. 96. See comments made under Reason/Answer Five.

John used this term "Lord's day" at a time when the Roman rulers were often deified. All inhabitants of the Roman Empire, including Christians, were called on to offer incense to the Roman gods or forfeit their lives. Local calendars included emperor days either to commemorate their birthdays or the time when they may have visited a city. Many times these "emperor days" took on religious significance. The emperor Domitian was "accustomed to call himself and to be called 'Lord and God.' "—Philip Schaff, *His-*

tory of the Christian Church, vol. 2, p. 44.

John had been banished to the Isle of Patmos during the reign of Domitian. During this imprisonment he received visions of Christ's kingdom of glory. He called Jesus "King of kings, and Lord of lords." Revelation 17:14; 19:16. Is it any wonder that he used the term "Lord's day" in Revelation 1:10 as he distinguished clearly who was truly the Lord worthy of worship?

It is more than interesting to remember that the four Gospels were all written many years after Christ ascended and that each Gospel refers to the seventh day (Saturday) as the Sabbath. If there was a new understanding after Christ's death, why didn't the Gospel writers make it known so that the Christian world would never have an occasion to doubt which day was the Sabbath?

Our questioner implies that the New Testament suggests no penalty for breaking the Sabbath.

But John wrote, "He that saith, I know him, and keepeth not his commandments, is a liar, and the truth is not in him." 1 John 2:4.

To be called a liar by God is penalty enough because we know that no unrepentant liar shall enter heaven: "All liars, shall have their part in the lake which burneth with fire and brimstone: which is the second death." Revelation 21:8.

Finally, we are told that we should walk in Jesus' steps: "He that saith he abideth in him ought himself also so to walk, even as He walked." 1 John 2:6. Where did Jesus go, or "walk," every Sabbath? "And he came to Nazareth, where he had been brought up: and, *as his custom was,* he went into the synagogue on the sabbath day." Luke 4:16.

"Fools for Christ?"

22. "My family and friends would call me a fool for keeping Saturday instead of Sunday."

ANSWER: Would we rather be called fools by God or by our fellowmen, whether they be family, friends, or foes?

Paul said: "We are fools for Christ's sake." 1 Corinthians 4:10.

I know we love our families and it would be a crushing blow if they should turn against us. But if God speaks to us through His Word and we reject Him because our families would turn against us, do we really love them? By faithfully obeying God we may eventually see them also accept the fullness of truth and receive our Lord's blessings.

The question is, Who should lead—those eager to serve God, or those hesitant to place God before earthly considerations?

I recommend highly the book by Helen K. Oswald called *That Book in the Attic*. You may get it by contacting the publisher of this book.

It relives the life of a young girl who, because of the anger and cruelty of her father, whom she loved and respected very much, had to leave home because she became a Sabbath keeper and joined the Seventh-day Adventist Church.

However, love won out, and she had the thrill of seeing her whole family accept the Sabbath truth she loved.

This story could be repeated by the thousands through the past century.

"Think not that I am come to send peace on earth: I came not to send peace, but a sword. For I am come to set a man at variance against his father, and the daughter against her mother, and the daughter in law against her mother in law. And a man's foes shall be they of his own household. He that loveth father or mother more than me is not worthy of me: and he that loveth son or daughter more than me is not worthy of me. And he that taketh not his cross, and followeth after me is not worthy of me. He that findeth his life shall lose it: and he that loseth his life for my sake shall find it." Matthew 10:34-39.

Regarding friends, how true are they if they would forsake you if you choose to be more faithful to Jesus? Remember, if you should lose a friend, you will be gaining many new

Sabbath-keeping friends in addition to the inner peace of knowing you are obeying Jesus.

Peter understood your question well, and he asked Jesus about it, "We have forsaken all, and followed thee; what shall we have therefore? And Jesus said unto them, . . . Every one that hath forsaken houses, or brethren, or sisters, or father, or mother, or wife, or children, or lands, for my name's sake, shall receive an hundredfold, and shall inherit everlasting life." Matthew 19:27-29.

Direct Revelation?

23. "God gave the Mormon Church a direct revelation that Sunday was substituted for the old Jewish Sabbath."

ANSWER: This reason is based on the following argument: "The observance of Sunday as the Lord's day comes to the Church of Jesus Christ of Latter-day Saints by direct appointment of the Lord by revelation to the head of the church in the present new dispensation of the gospel; and that revelation transforms the 'probability,' that the first day of the week was substituted for the old Jewish Sabbath, into a certainty."—"The Lord's Day," a tract by Elder Brigham H. Roberts.

A Christian should never accept the kind of reason given here, for no true prophet will speak contrary to the inspired Bible.

The angel who came to Joseph Smith, the man who was supposed to have had this direct revelation, had to be an evil angel; no angel of light would instruct a person to go against the Bible. We learned in earlier pages that neither God, Jesus, angels, the prophets, nor the apostles changed the day of worship from the seventh day of the week to the first day. The Roman Catholic Church admits the attempted change; so why search further (Look again at our answer to Reason/Answer 4) and the Bible predicted this attempted change (see Daniel 7:25).

We are warned that in the last days many false prophets

will arise: "And many false prophets shall rise, and shall deceive many.... For there shall arise false Christs, and false prophets, and shall shew great signs and wonders; insomuch that, if it were possible, they shall deceive the very elect." Matthew 24:11, 24.

The best way to test a prophet or spirit is with the Word of God: "To the law and to the testimony: if they speak not according to this word, it is because there is no light in them." Isaiah 8:20.

"Beloved, believe not every spirit, but try the spirits whether they are of God: because many false prophets are gone out into the world." 1 John 4:1.

While in Illinois Joseph Smith, the Mormon prophet, was supposed to have received direct revelations from the angel Moroni. These unfolding concepts differed widely from generally accepted orthodox views, whether Catholic or Protestant, such as, "The Father has a body of flesh and bones as tangible as man's; the Son also; but the Holy Ghost has not a body of flesh and bones, but is a personage of Spirit.... Nor is God outside time."

In an 1844 funeral oration Smith said, "God himself was once as we are now, and *is an exalted man,* and sits enthroned in yonder heavens! That is the great secret. If the vail were rent today, ... you would see him like a man in form....

"We have imagined and supposed that God *was God from all eternity. I will refute that idea....* It is the first principle of the Gospel to know for certainty the *character of God,* ... that *he was once a man like us,* ... and you have got to be gods yourselves, and to be kings and priests to God, the same as all Gods have done before you."—Jerome L. Clark, *1844: Religious Movements* (Nashville: Southern Publishing Association, 1968), vol. 1, pp. 120, 121.

Although these words are not written primarily to expose Joseph Smith as a false prophet, the reader should be aware of an alleged prophet's relationship to the Bible.

Paul was clear: "But though we, or an angel from heaven,

preach any other gospel unto you than that which we have preached unto you, let him be accursed." Galatians 1:8.

Nothing Specific About the Seventh Day

24. "There is no commandment in the Ten Commandments which says that we are to keep the seventh day of the week."

ANSWER: This reason is in a letter that the Billy Graham Evangelistic Association has sent, from time to time, to those who raise the Sabbath-Sunday issue.

Part of the letter reads: "In his book, *Practical and Perplexing Questions Answered,* R. A. Torrey suggests that there is no commandment in the Ten Commandments which says that we are to keep the seventh day of the week. The words 'of the week' are added by man to the commandment as given by God. What God really commanded through Moses was: 'Six days shalt thou labor and do all thy work, but the seventh day is the sabbath of the Lord thy God.' It does not say 'the seventh day of the week' but rather 'the seventh day after six days of labor.' Whether it should be the seventh day of the week or the first day of the week depends upon whether one is a Jew or a Christian. Whether we keep the seventh day of the week or the first day of the week, we are keeping the Fourth Commandment to the letter. If one is a Jew belonging to the old creation, let him keep the seventh day of the week, but if he is a Christian and on resurrection ground, let him keep the first day of the week, resurrection day."

This letter misses the point: The commandment does not say "Remember the seventh day after six days of labor to keep it holy," but plainly "Remember the sabbath day, to keep it holy." The commandment does not provide an option to choose any seventh day after a six-day work period, whereby any day of the week could serve as the Sabbath of the fourth commandment.

The fourth commandment does make clear that the Sabbath was a specific day, recurring every seventh day, in commemoration of Creation week. See Genesis 2:1-3. The manna experience (see Exodus 16:23-26) emphasized the specificity of that unchangeable seventh day (see Reason/Answer One). It was *the* sabbath day that was blessed, the seventh day commemorating the six days of Creation, not any other day that may follow a six-day work period. See again Exodus 20:11.

Thus to say that a Sabbath keeper or a Sunday keeper "is keeping the Fourth Commandment to the letter" is incorrect. Such a statement rests on the premise rejected above that the Sabbath commandment allows Christians to keep any seventh day, whenever it falls in the week.

Christian Liberty

25. "Although no biblical command requires Christians to keep Sunday, its observance is the Christian's liberty to enjoy."

ANSWER: Earlier reasons/answers, such as Three, Four, and Five, have established the fact that the first part of the above reason is true: There is no basis in the New Testament for the observance of Sunday as the Sabbath.

We now turn to Galatians 5:13 to discover what Paul meant by Christian liberty: "For, brethren, ye have been called unto liberty; only use not liberty for an occasion to the flesh, but by love serve one another."

What does "called unto liberty" mean? Surely, it doesn't mean "called unto license." Paul is not advocating that a Christian may do as he pleases. But "called unto license" is what a person gets into when he chooses his own day of worship, contrary to the law of God.

The Bible makes clear that Christians are not free to sin: "Therefore to him that knoweth to do good, and doeth it not, to him it is sin." James 4:17. Consequently, "called unto liberty" is not a call to sin or to live above law.

It is just as wrong to break the Sabbath as it is to worship and bow down to idols, take God's name in vain, dishonor one's parents, kill, commit adultery, steal, lie, or covet. The Bible says it is: "For whosoever shall keep the whole law, and yet offend in one point, he is guilty of all. . . . So speak ye, and so do, as they that shall be judged by the law of liberty." James 2:10-12.

Why does James call the Ten Commandments the "law of liberty"? Because when we break the law, we come under the condemnation of the law. When we are keeping the law by God's grace, we are at liberty. Christians have been set free from the bondage of sin. See Romans 6:6-18. When we walk "after the Spirit," we are "free from the law of sin and death." Romans 8:4, 2.

Citizens of the United States take pride in living in the "land of the free and the home of the brave." As long as they keep the laws of the land, they are "free"; but if they break such laws, they are soon in jail, in bondage. The free citizen obeys the law. The obedient citizen, not the lawbreaker, is "called unto liberty."

But what did Paul mean in Galatians 5:13 regarding the Christian's liberty? In Galatians 5, Paul had been talking about the primary problem that had been confusing the Galatians—whether circumcision and Jewish ceremonial laws were mandatory for salvation. Paul's argument was simple: The liberty of salvation by faith in Christ freed the Christians, Jew and Gentile alike, from the burden and meaninglessness of circumcision as a requirement for salvation.

The Christian Galatian who thought circumcision was necessary to salvation was in bondage as much as the pagan Galatian who still worshiped his idols, remaining under the bondage of righteousness by ritualism.

Righteousness by faith in Jesus Christ includes works but not the works of ritualism that the Galatians were involved in. "Works" that flow from the grateful heart are the works of obedience and trust and produce the "fruit of the Spirit" Galatians 5:22, 23. Obedience to known duty is the inevitable result of faith (Romans 1:5; 16:26; James 4:17) and is summed up in one word, love (Romans 13:10; Galatians 5:6).

Again we return to a theme emphasized frequently in this book. Jesus said it often, "If ye love me, keep my commandments." John 14:15. John repeated His Master's counsel, "He that saith, I know him, and keepeth not his commandments, is a liar, and the truth is not in him." 1 John 2:4. "By this we know that we love the children of God, when we love God, and keep his commandments. For this is the love of God, that we keep his commandments: and his commandments are not grievous." 1 John 5:2, 3.

A Personal Note

This book was not meant to be a sterile theological argument. Far from it! Each page, and much more could have been said, has developed out of experience. I have seen the happy results in the lives of thousands who have grasped the Sabbath truth. For some it came easily; others needed more time. But, with all, the refrain is the same: Thanks for the effort that it took. Thanks for the blessed experience of Sabbath worship. Thanks for the joy that Sabbath keeping has brought to my family.

God is calling out a people who will joyfully keep His law, including the seventh-day Sabbath. Revelation 14:6-12. John refers to this worldwide call as "the everlasting gospel." Verse 6. The consistent message of God regarding sin and salvation, understood clearly by both Old and New Testament writers, constitutes "the everlasting gospel."

The appeal in these last days is urgent—"The hour of his judgment is come" (Verse 7). Its message is clear—"Worship him that made heaven and earth, and the sea, and the fountains of waters" (Verse 7). Here again we hear the call for Sabbath worship and obedience to that fourth commandment, which reminds us that the seventh-day Sabbath was given as a weekly reminder of our Creator and of how the world began.

Those who respond to "the everlasting gospel," with its gifts and obligations, are described as those who "keep the commandments of God, and the faith of Jesus." Revelation 14:12.

Listening to God is serious business. Rejecting His Word leads down a self-destructing path.

The psalmist said it well for all of us: "I have chosen the way of truth: thy judgments have I laid before me. I have stuck unto thy testimonies: O Lord, put me not to shame. I will run the way of thy commandments, when thou shalt enlarge my heart." Psalm 119:30-32.